Thanksgiving Rules

Laurie
Friedman

ILLUSTRATED BY
Teresa Murfin

CAROLRHODA BOOKS MINNEAPOLIS • NEW YORK

For my mother, who makes Thanksgiving
and every other day a celebration

I love you, L.B.F.

For Elaine and all my family
across the pond —T.M.

Text copyright © 2009 by Laurie B. Friedman
Illustrations copyright © 2009 by Teresa Murfin

Carolrhoda Books
A division of Lerner Publishing Group, Inc.
241 First Avenue North
Minneapolis, MN 55401 U.S.A.

Website address: www.lernerbooks.com

Library of Congress Cataloging-in-Publication Data

Friedman, Laurie B.
        Thanksgiving rules / by Laurie Friedman ; illustrations by Teresa Murfin.
               p.   cm.
        Summary: Young Percy Isaac Gifford provides a list of ten rules for getting
the most out of Thanksgiving Day, especially how best to enjoy the buffet.
        ISBN 978-0-8225-7983-0 (lib. bdg. : alk. paper)
        [1. Stories in rhyme. 2. Thanksgiving Day—Fiction. 3. Rules (Philosophy)—
Fiction. 4. Family life—Fiction.] I. Murfin, Teresa, ill. II. Title.
PZ8.3.F9116Thd 2009
[E]—dc22   2008038047

Manufactured in the United States of America
4 – DP – 10/15/10

I'm Percy Isaac Gifford.

Today's **Thanksgiving** Day.

**This is
my empty
stomach.**

**This is the
buffet.**

Thanksgiving Party

me

yum yum

Buffet

By Percy Isaac Gifford
(P.I.G.)

And here's a little secret:
I'm a *Thanksgiving Pro.*
When it comes to turkey day,
there's nothing I don't know.

I get the most out of my holiday.
I promise, you can too.
Just follow my simple rules.
That's all you have to do.

**The first thing you must know:
moms like to set** *a Mood.*
**They like to control everything
from your clothing to the food.**

So wear whatever you have to,
from your head down to your feet.
Remember, the sooner you get dressed,
the sooner you can eat.

Next, you have to get involved.
Dad likes when I volunteer.
He says seeing me help out
fills his heart with cheer.

Rule 2:
Eat, drink
but first
CLEAN!

Now, I know that it's no fun
to sweep or clean or peel.
But trust me when I tell you,
it's the fastest way to the meal.

After you're done cleaning,
I'm sure you'll want to EAT.
But you can't do that just yet.
First, you have to greet.

That means when family or friends
arrive, you have to be polite.
But here's a helpful tip:
it doesn't have to take all night.

I'm talking about an art form
I call *The Quick Hello*.
A simple, friendly greeting,
and then you're good to go.

The place you should be heading
is what I call *The Main Event.*
It's best to get there early.
For directions: follow the scent.

Now, please take a moment
and savor this part of your day.
For my friend,
you have arrived at the. . .

Here's where I can be most helpful.
It's time to *fill your plate*.
Remember, the round thing in your
hand can hold a lot of weight.

Start with piles of turkey.
It's best when nice and hot.
Then pour on a little gravy.
Better yet, pour on a lot.

From there, you'll want to add
a little something on the side.
This part can be tricky.
Stick with me. I'll be your guide.

figure 1

figure 2

First, take sweet potatoes.
Trust me, they taste good.
Don't be afraid of stuffing,
even though it looks like wood.

figure 3

figure 4

Definitely try the green beans.
For color, add cranberry sauce.
If you don't eat all of these,
it will be your loss.

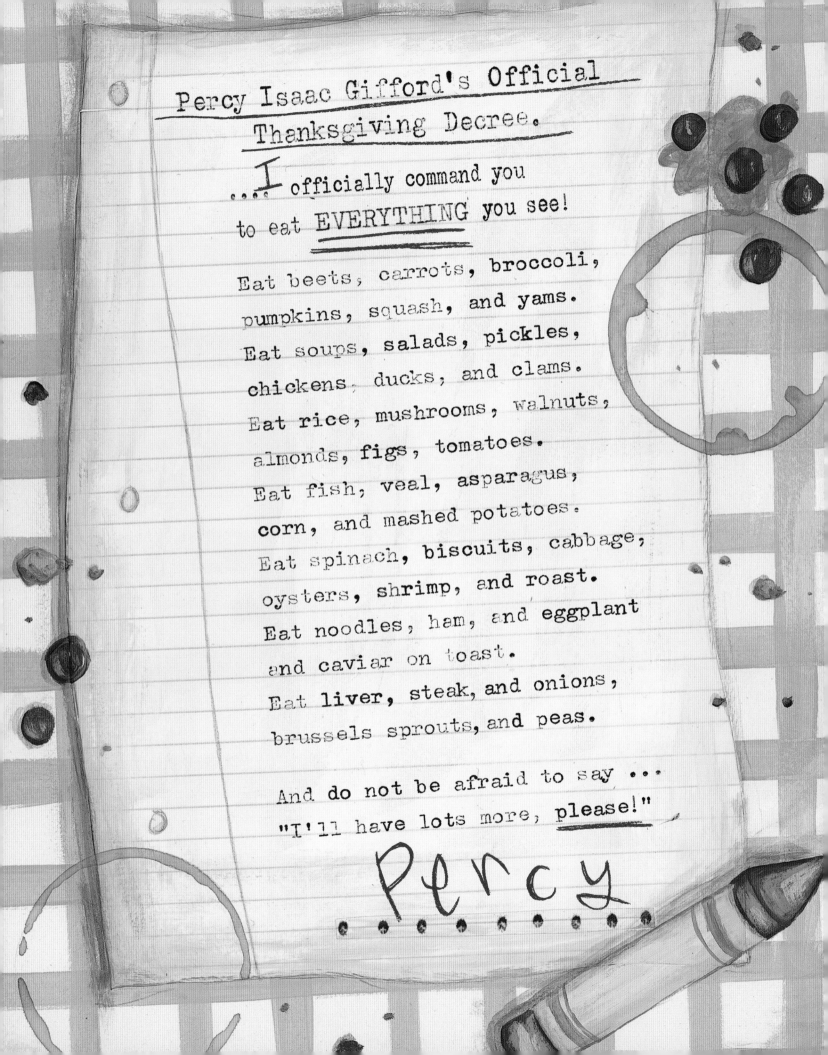

Percy Isaac Gifford's Official Thanksgiving Decree.

.....I officially command you
to eat EVERYTHING you see!

Eat beets, carrots, broccoli,
pumpkins, squash, and yams.
Eat soups, salads, pickles,
chickens, ducks, and clams.
Eat rice, mushrooms, walnuts,
almonds, figs, tomatoes.
Eat fish, veal, asparagus,
corn, and mashed potatoes.
Eat spinach, biscuits, cabbage,
oysters, shrimp, and roast.
Eat noodles, ham, and eggplant
and caviar on toast.
Eat liver, steak, and onions,
brussels sprouts, and peas.

And do not be afraid to say ...
"I'll have lots more, please!"

Percy

Your plate should now be close to full,
though hopefully there are holes.
My advice: plug them up
with piles of dinner rolls.

Rule # 7:
Don't stop or drop.
Just take some rolls.

My friend, you've now got what you need.
Go find a place to sit.
It's time to gobble up your dinner.
EAT EVERY SINGLE BIT!

**Eat till your plate is squeaky clean.
Then go back for more.
The *second time around*
is something I adore.**

DESSERT!

Sampling some of everything
really cannot hurt.
You should try each type of pie.
Taste every tart or cake.
Show that you *appreciate*
everyone who tried to bake.

And while we're on the subject,
appreciation's a *big deal*.
Today's a day to show you're thankful,
and not just for the meal.

It's a day to show your loved ones
just what they mean to you.
So before Thanksgiving is over,
there's something I like to do.

I give everyone around me
their own Thanksgiving hug.
I call it the Percy Isaac Special,
which means it's BIG and SNUG!

Almost everyone seems to like it.
They almost always say, *"How nice."*

But I must admit that over the years,
I've been given some advice.

Once or twice, it's been suggested
that I modify my technique. . . .

So I now provide the
Overeaters' Special—
a simple, light peck on the cheek.